To Emily

From..............................

It was Christmas Eve and Emily
was snug and warm in her cozy bed.
She was trying so hard to go to sleep.
But she could hear strange noises.

It wasn't the sound of sleigh bells.
It wasn't the sound of reindeer hoofs on the roof.
It wasn't even the sound of Santa unpacking his sack.

It was more of a

HARRUMPH!

and an

OOF!

It was no use.

There'd be no sleep for Emily
until she'd found out what
was making that noise.

Emily crept down the stairs and peered into the living room. There were three stockings hanging from the fireplace.

One of them belonged
to Emily. But where had
the other two come from?
Suddenly, a muffled voice
came from the chimney.

"Oh, dear.
I'm even
more
stuck now!"

There was a scuffling sound
from behind the Christmas
tree, and Emily jumped
as a small elf appeared.

"Uh, hello," said the elf. "I guess you've caught us!"

Emily listened as the elf explained
that Santa was stuck in the chimney.
The elf had tried to pull him out. But the
only things that had come down so far
were Santa's boots and pants!

"I can help you," suggested Emily. "I'll hold
Santa's feet and we can both pull."
The elf agreed. "Between us, we might be
able to get him unstuck."

Emily grasped both of Santa's feet firmly. But, just at that moment, a light went on upstairs. "Emily, is that you?" called her mom. "Back to bed now, please, or Santa won't come!"

At that exact moment,
Santa shot back up
the chimney... with
Emily still hanging
onto his feet.

The poor elf could not believe his eyes.
But there was no time to think...
Emily's mom was coming
out of her bedroom.

"I'm coming!" squeaked the elf. He hurried
up the stairs and jumped into Emily's bed,
pulling the covers up over his head.
"Night-night, sweetie!" said Emily's
mom through the doorway.

Meanwhile, up on the roof, Santa and Emily had landed in a heap. The clever reindeer had hooked their reins under Santa's arms and pulled as hard as they could.

"Good job!" said Santa, brushing himself down. "No more cookies for me tonight!"

Emily scrambled to her feet. But Santa
was so busy, he didn't notice that Emily
and the elf had traded places!

"I think we'd better deliver the rest of the
presents first," said Santa, "and leave this
house for last."

Santa climbed into the driver's seat.

"Elf, you get the presents ready for our next destination," he called over his shoulder. "But I'm not Elf…" replied Emily.

Santa wasn't really listening.
He was talking to the reindeer.
"Up, up, and away!" Santa called,
and the reindeer took off before
Emily had time to explain.

Emily held on tight as the
sleigh climbed high into the
night sky, above the rooftops.

Surrounded by sacks, Emily was so busy figuring out which presents were which, there was no time to let Santa know that there'd been a mistake.

There were **big**
presents for the cities,

and **SHINY** presents
for the towns.

There were **ODD**-shaped
presents for the villages,

and **mystery**
presents for the farms.

To Emily

As they landed at their next stop,
Santa decided that he couldn't risk
getting stuck in a chimney again.

"Elf, I think you'd better make the
deliveries from now on," decided Santa,
"while I sort the presents."

Emily *shimmied* down chimneys.

She **squeezed** through cat flaps.

And, if all else failed, she used Santa's *magic* key to let herself in.

In each house, Emily picked up the cookies to take home to Mrs. Claus, and carrots for the reindeer.

Finally, there was just one sack left, and
Santa still hadn't realized his mistake!
The sleigh headed back over the
rooftops to Emily's house.

To
Emily

Emily had never had so much
fun as when she slid down her
own chimney with a sack of
her own presents!

She put her presents under
the Christmas tree, then picked
up Santa's pants and boots
and put them in the sack.

"Psst! Elf, where are you?" whispered Emily.

A very happy Elf appeared, rubbing his eyes.
"I've had such a lovely nap," he said.
Emily handed over the sack
and waved as Elf
disappeared up
the chimney.

Back in her cozy bed, Emily listened
to the sounds of reindeer hoofs on
the roof, sleigh bells, and, very faintly,

"Ho ho ho!

Merry Christmas!"

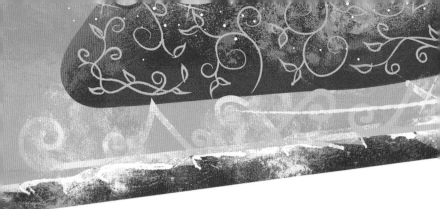

Or was that,

"Ho ho ho!
yummy cookies!"?

Write your name on the gift tags.

Draw yourself as an elf.

Create one-of-a-kind books for any child on Put Me In The Story!

visit → www.putmeinthestory.com/morenames

- Find *Unique Gifts* for birthdays, holidays, or any day
- Personalize this and other great stories with *Any Child's Name*
- Choose from over *100 Personalized* versions of bestselling children's books